The Kids in Mrs. Z's Class

Emma McKenna, Full Out

The Kids in Mrs. Z's Class

Emma McKenna, Full Out

KATE MESSNER

illustrated by **KAT FAJARDO**

ALGONQUIN YOUNG READERS
WORKMAN PUBLISHING
NEW YORK

Copyright © 2024 by Kate Messner
Illustration copyright © 2024 by Kat Fajardo
Cover art color and interior shading by Pablo A. Castro
Kraft paper texture © klyaksun/Shutterstock
Paw print © pingebat/Shutterstock

Algonquin Young Readers
Workman Publishing
Hachette Book Group, Inc.
1290 Avenue of the Americas
New York, NY 10104
workman.com

Algonquin Young Readers is an imprint of Workman Publishing, a division of Hachette Book Group, Inc. The Workman name and logo are registered trademarks of Hachette Book Group, Inc.

Design by Neil Swaab

Library of Congress Cataloging-in-Publication Data is available.
ISBN 978-1-5235-2571-3 (hardcover)
ISBN 978-1-5235-2572-0 (paperback)

First Edition May 2024 LSC-C
Printed in the USA on responsibly sourced paper.

10 9 8 7 6 5 4 3 2 1

For my friends at Brookdale Elementary, Carl Allgrove School, Granada Hills Charter School, Greenbriar Elementary, Hill Elementary, Independent School District 196, Northeast Elementary, Old Hundred Elementary, Orchard School, R.D. Seymour School, and Shaker Road Elementary. And for Adrianna. Thanks to all of you for your help!

MEET
The Kids in Mrs. Z's Class

Adam

Ayana

Carlota

Emma

Fia

Lucy

Mars

Memo

Olive

Chapter 1
Ready? Okay!

Emma McKenna put on leggings and a bright orange shirt.

Nope.

She put on her cheer outfit.

Nope.

She put on purple shorts, a black tee, and her rainbow hoodie.

Nope. Nope. Nope.

She needed a first-day-of-school outfit that made her look interesting and fun.

An outfit that said, "Here is someone cool to be friends with!"

An outfit that said, "There is no reason whatsoever to make fun of this nice person or their tired old dog, even if he does have a weird, wrinkly Yoda face."

Emma put her cheer outfit back on. It didn't say any of the things she was hoping for, but it was the best she could do. She went downstairs and grabbed a banana for breakfast.

"Can I have your peel?" asked Abby.

"No, it's my turn!" said Mae. She snatched it, dropped it, stepped on it, and flailed her arms. "Whoooooa!" Then she crashed dramatically to the floor.

Slipping on banana peels was the twins' favorite thing, ever since Dad showed them an old TV show about three men who spent all day smashing cream pies in people's faces and slipping on banana peels. Four-year-olds and dads thought weird things were funny.

"Hey, what's today?" asked Abby.

"Tuesday," said Mom, who was just coming downstairs.

"National Skyscraper Day," said Emma. She loved unusual holidays as much as the twins loved banana peels.

"Can we go see a skyscraper?" Abby asked.

Emma shook her head. "There are no sky-scrapers in Peppermint Falls. But we can build a block tower later."

A car horn beeped outside.

"Dad's waiting." Mom blew Emma a kiss. "Have a great first day!"

"You're quiet today, Emma Bemma." Dad liked to make up rhymes for everyone's name. Except for Mom, who told him a long time ago that if he called her Lydia Squidia one more time she'd pop him in the nose. "Are you nervous?"

"Not really." Emma looked out the window as they passed her old school. This year, she was starting third grade at a brand-new school called Curiosity Academy.

"It's all right to feel jittery," Dad said. "Especially since you don't know the kids in your class."

"I'm more excited than nervous." It was true that Emma didn't really know any of her classmates. That meant she wouldn't have friends right away. But it also meant she wouldn't have enemies. And that was more important.

"All set?" Dad pulled into the drop-off circle.

"Yep!" Emma got out of the car and walked up the steps to the big double doors. Then she paused for a moment.

READY? OKAY!

That was how Coach Kayla taught them to start cheers. Thinking it helped Emma feel ready for other things, too.

She took a deep breath and stepped inside.

Mrs. Z's room was upstairs at the end of the hall. It had big-kid desks pushed together to make tables. It had a whiteboard up front and a cage on the windowsill with a fluffy guinea pig named Honey. It had a Choice Time area where you could build robots or write stories or look at things under a microscope.

Best of all, it had Mrs. Z.

Her real name was Mrs. Zamora, but everyone called her Mrs. Z. Emma loved how zippy that sounded. She loved how Mrs. Z had called her students "curiosity seekers" and "problem solvers" at the summer open house. She loved

Mrs. Z's bright orange sneakers and her fun science jewelry. Today, her earrings were dangly dragonflies.

"Hello, Emma!" Mrs. Z's dragonflies sparkled in the light. "Find your seat and we'll get this day started."

Emma found her name card. Her table neighbors, Poppy, Rohan, and Olive, were just arriving, too.

Poppy's backpack had colorful key chains hanging off the zippers. Rohan's had a cartoon shark with a briefcase under its fin. Olive's schoolbag looked homemade, with patches of fabric sewn on like a collage.

"Hi!" Emma smiled her best cheer smile. Rohan and Poppy said hi back, and Olive gave a quiet wave.

Emma liked them already.

There were maybe-friends filling in other

tables, too. Emma remembered Thunder and Carlota from the open house. She recognized a quiet boy named Steven who'd been there as well.

Also Memo, but now his leg was in a cast. Emma hoped she'd get to sign it. She'd always wanted to break something so people could sign her cast.

"All right, friends," Mrs. Z. said. "Let's talk about our classroom community." She went over the rules and announced some fun third-grade activities.

The Daily Scribble was when everyone wrote for *exactly* five minutes. Mrs. Z set a timer that looked like an egg.

"We'll have special classes every week. There's art, gym, library, and music." Mrs. Z put a schedule on the board.

The only class Emma cared about was

music. In third grade you got to play an instrument. Emma was going to choose flute. Last summer she'd gone to a jazz festival with Mom, and the lady who played flute made it sound like a super-happy bird.

Tweedle-lee-deet!

Tweedle-lee-deet-deet!

Tweedle-lee-deedle-lee-deet-deet-deeeeeee!

"Well, hello there!" Mrs. Z said to someone at the back of the room. Emma was still looking at the specials schedule. They probably wouldn't give out flutes the first day. Maybe by the end of the week. That was okay. She could practice all weekend.

"Sorry I'm late," the person said.

Emma froze in her seat. She knew that voice.

It was the last person in the world she wanted to see.

Chapter 2
Anyone but Lucy

No. No. No. It couldn't be Lucy.

Lucy wasn't going to Curiosity Academy. She hadn't been at the open house. This late person only *sounded* like Lucy.

That was possible, right?

Emma turned around.

"Where should I sit?" asked the person, who had not only Lucy's voice but also Lucy's pigtails, Lucy's overalls, and Lucy's shark tooth necklace.

Also Lucy's big blue eyes, which got bigger when they landed on Emma.

"Can I go to the nurse?" Lucy blurted.

"What's wrong?" Mrs. Z asked.

"I NEED TO GO TO THE NURSE."

Mrs. Z raised her eyebrows and hurried Lucy to the door. She turned back to the class and pointed to the board. "Go ahead and start the Daily Scribble."

The Daily Scribble
for Tuesday, September 3

what are you most looking forward to this year?

Five minutes ago, Emma could have answered that question just fine.

Not anymore. Lucy ruined everything.

I am looking forward to my new classroom.

Not with Lucy in it.

I am looking forward to learning to play flute.

What if Lucy chose flute, too?

I am looking forward to moving up a level in cheerleading. I can do back handsprings now. Last year I could only do cartwheels.

Emma sighed. Cartwheels were what got her an enemy in the first place.

I am looking forward to going home to see my dog.

Emma looked at the clock. It was only 10 a.m. Five more hours to go.

After the Daily Scribble, everyone got to share One Interesting Thing about themselves.

Fia had just moved to Peppermint Falls from Trinidad.

Steven helped his grandmother care for injured animals.

Mars wanted to be a makeup artist for scary movies when he grew up, and Ruthie wanted to be a Broadway star.

Emma didn't know what she wanted to be. Was she supposed to know that?

Poppy spoke Cantonese.

Adam spoke Urdu *and* Arabic.

Carlota volunteered at a center to help new immigrants.

Emma stared down at her skirt. Was

cheerleading interesting? Maybe not.

She had twin sisters. That was kind of interesting.

She had a pet bulldog so old he had to go for walks in a baby stroller. That was interesting, but Emma couldn't share it. Not without reminding Lucy of the nickname.

"I . . . uh . . . like cheerleading," Emma said, when it was her turn.

Mrs. Z nodded and smiled. Then she moved on to Thunder, who told the class that she knew how to speak hamster and was teaching her dog English using buttons with words on them.

There was no doubt about it. Emma was the Least Interesting Person in Mrs. Z's class. No one would want to be friends with her. Third grade was doomed.

"Doomed" was a good word. When you

used it, grown-ups always said you were exaggerating, but Emma wasn't. She knew doom when she saw it coming.

There was more doom at lunchtime. Where was Emma supposed to sit?

The first table she passed was mostly boys. Memo motioned her over. "This is the dragons' table. Are you a dragon?"

Was she? An Interesting Person would say yes, but Emma felt like she needed more information. "Maybe tomorrow."

Theo nodded. "We will be here every day, guarding the treasure."

Emma ended up sitting with Rohan, Poppy, Sebastian, and Olive. They were all more interesting than she was.

Rohan wanted to be a businessman someday. One who also saved the Earth.

Poppy had a very cool lunchbox and also two parakeets at home.

Sebastian had stray cats in his yard.

And Olive had chickens. They laid eggs and everything. "Do you have pets?" she asked Emma.

"A French bulldog." Emma didn't tell them Bongo's name because what if someone mentioned it to Lucy and she told everybody about the mean nickname she'd given Emma last year?

By the end of the day, Emma was exhausted. It was a lot of work to make sure you didn't say anything to remind your enemy why you were enemies.

"I'll see you tomorrow." Mrs. Z high-fived everyone as they left. "It's going to be another great day!"

Emma held up her hand and got her high five, but she wasn't convinced.

Another day in the same class as Lucy? There was nothing great about that.

Chapter 3
Delicious Mistakes and Interesting Ideas

After school, Emma walked down the street to Minnie's, the ice cream shop her parents owned. She loved looking in all the shop windows. Her favorites were Doomscroll Comics, ZaZa's Pizza, and the music store called Lintowongan. They often had flutes in the window.

The bells on the ice cream shop door jingled when Emma stepped inside. Aunt Cassie was working today, and she always let Emma help.

Sometimes Emma sorted silverware or wiped counters, but her favorite job was eating mistakes. Like when a person ordered vanilla ice cream but the scooper accidentally made a cookie dough cone instead.

It was an important job. You couldn't just throw out the mistakes. That was wasteful, and Emma cared about the planet.

"Hey, kiddo!" said Aunt Cassie. "Want to refill napkin containers?"

"Sure!"

"How was school?"

"Okay," Emma said, "except that I have an enemy."

"On the very first day?" Aunt Cassie gave Emma's shoulder a squeeze. "Want to talk about it?"

"No thanks." Grown-ups never understood friend trouble. They always said you should go talk to the person. Easy-peasy. As if you could just walk up to them and do that without them calling you mean names in front of everybody and insulting your dog, too.

Emma was finishing with the napkins when Mom showed up with the twins.

"How was your first day?" Mom asked. "Do you love it?"

"It was fine," Emma said.

"Do you have friends yet?" Mae asked.

"Nope. But I have an enemy."

"What a memonee?" asked Abby.

"*Enemy*," Emma said. "It's a friend who doesn't like you anymore."

"Oooohhh," the twins said together. At least someone understood how bad this was.

"Is this about Lucy?" Mom asked.

Emma didn't want to talk about it. "I have to go to cheer now," she said.

"Hey, everybody!" Dad walked in with a basket of bananas. Abby made a grab for them. "Hands off! These are for splits."

The twins ran off, and Emma grabbed her cheer bag.

"Give me a minute," Dad said as he wiped a counter.

Emma sighed. She hated being late for cheer. Sometimes she wished her parents had never bought the ice cream shop.

"Oops!" said Aunt Cassie. "I accidentally scooped mint chocolate chip instead of vanilla."

Mom put her hands on her hips. "Those flavors look nothing alike. They aren't even next to each other in the freezer."

"These things happen." Aunt Cassie shrugged and winked at Emma, who took her cone and headed to the car.

"You're eating our profits," Dad said.

"I'm saving the Earth," Emma said, and slurped up a sweet minty lick of mistake.

Coach Kayla was just starting practice when they got to the gym. "Let's warm up, team!" she shouted.

Emma joined everyone on the mat to stretch with butterfly legs. She did her warm-up handstands. She tried a split but couldn't get all the way down.

"Great job, Emma Zemma!" Dad shouted. He never brought a laptop or a book like other parents. He just watched and cheered every time Emma did anything. Whether she did it well or not.

It was extra hard for her to concentrate today. She needed to make friends at school before Lucy told everyone to call her Bongo

Butt. How could she do that when all her new classmates were so much more interesting than she was?

"Let's try the beginning of our new routine," Coach Kayla called. "Bases! Make sure you get to your spots on time."

Bases were people like Emma who were in charge of lifting up other people, called flyers. During a stunt, bases worked together to lift the flyer off the ground and keep her safe while she struck a pose up there. Being a base was a big job. Even bigger than eating mistakes.

"Ready? Okay!"

"One, two, three, four, five, six, seven, eight!" Coach Kayla counted out the beats. Emma did a back walkover and clapped her hands to her sides. Then she ran to her spot for the stunt.

"Nice job, Emma Supremma!" Dad shouted after the bases lowered their flyer back to the mat.

"Now let's try it full out!" called Coach Kayla.

"Full out" meant putting everything together. All the tumbling moves and dance steps and stunts. With one hundred percent energy. It was Emma's favorite way to do everything.

"Great!" shouted Coach Kayla when they finished. "How many of you are staying for open gym?"

"I can't tonight," Emma said. "I promised my sisters we'd build a tower for National Skyscraper Day."

"National Skyscraper Day is a thing?" asked Anna, who was in seventh grade. "I had no idea!"

"That's so interesting," said her friend Alex.

"Yep." Emma liked knowing something the middle school girls didn't. "Next week is Chocolate Milkshake Day. We're having a special at the ice cream shop."

"Minnie's?" Alex's face lit up. "I love that place!"

"My parents own it," Emma said. Maybe that should have been her Interesting Thing.

"What other days are there?" asked Anna.

"Let's see . . . there's Penguin Awareness Day, Lost Sock Memorial Day, and National No Pants Day."

"That's hilarious!" said Anna.

"So *interesting*!" Alex said again.

Was it? Emma thought about that.

Maybe she had a way to make friends with her interesting new classmates after all.

Chapter 4
Every Day a Holiday

The second day of school was Eat an Extra Dessert Day, and Emma had a plan. A few plans, actually.

Plan A was to invite everyone in her class to Minnie's after school to eat mistakes. But that plan fell apart when Emma found out Mom would be working instead of Aunt Cassie. Mom didn't scoop mistakes. They'd be lucky if they each got one drip.

Plan B was to make cookies. They were out

of flour, though, and there wasn't time to go to the store after dinner.

But there *was* time for Emma to count the gummy worms in the stash of birthday candy under her bed.

That was plan C.

There were eighteen gummy worms. Emma had been hoping for nineteen so she'd have one for everybody, including her and Mrs. Z. But eighteen would be okay.

Actually, eighteen was even better. Then Emma could offer Mrs. Z the last gummy worm instead of eating it herself. Mrs. Z would say, "Holy cow, Emma! You *are* interesting. And kind, too!" Everyone would agree, and then there was no way they'd go along with Lucy's mean nickname.

"Good morning, curiosity seekers!" said Mrs. Z. "I'd like to tell you about a special assembly happening next week. Because this is a new school, we need new traditions. We need a school color and—"

"Purple!" shouted Synclaire.

"Pink!" said Ayana.

"Yellow!" called Fia. "Or green! Or blue!"

Mrs. Z raised her eyebrows.

"Rainbow!" said Thunder.

"That's actually not a color," said Sebastian.

"It's all the colors," Thunder said. "That way none of them feels bad."

"Friends!" Mrs. Z clapped her hands three times. "We're not picking a color now. But we *are* going to choose an animal for our school mascot. First we'll vote in our classroom next week. Then the top three ideas from each class will be presented at the assembly."

Emma snuck a glance at Lucy. This assembly probably wouldn't involve angry coleslaw or underwear, but you never knew. Emma wasn't going anywhere near that stage. It had doom written all over it.

Art class also started out doomed because Lucy and Emma got put at the same table. But as soon as that happened, Lucy asked to go to the nurse. Emma ended up sitting by Rohan instead.

When Mrs. Fletcher, the art teacher, told them to sketch the animal they thought should be the school mascot, Rohan drew a fox. A really good one.

"That's amazing!" said Emma.

"Thanks!" said Rohan. "What are you going to draw?"

"Umm . . . maybe a pig?" That was the

only animal Emma knew how to draw. Aunt Cassie had taught her an easy way, using three circles.

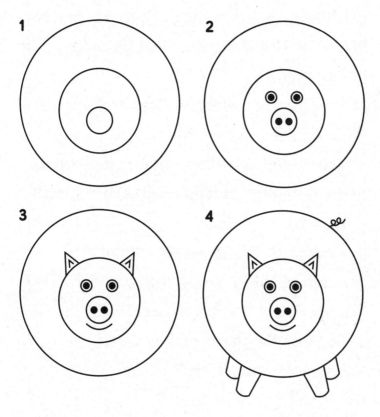

Emma didn't really think the mascot should be a pig, but that was okay. She had more important things on her mind. Like Operation Gummy Worm.

When it was time for lunch, Emma tucked her bag of gummy worms into her pocket. She waited until everyone had finished eating to pull them out.

"Happy Eat an Extra Dessert Day!" She dropped a red one on Poppy's tray.

"Uh . . . thanks?" Poppy didn't look excited to eat a gummy worm that had been in Emma's grubby hand. Emma had just washed them, but Poppy didn't know that. Shoot.

Emma held a worm out to Sebastian. "Happy Eat an Extra Dessert Day!"

"Why do they have gummy *worms*?" he said. "Why not gummy cockroaches or gummy fruit flies?"

Rohan laughed.

Emma did not. Suddenly, the sticky wad

of gummy worms in her hand smelled a lot like doom. "Did you know that tomorrow is Cheese Pizza Day and also Be Late for Something Day?"

"There should be a National New Ideas Day," said Rohan, "where everyone tries to think out of the box."

"Tomorrow should be National Bake Cupcakes Day!" said Poppy.

"Or National Nailed-It Day," said Sebastian. "That's a day when you try to make cupcakes that look like the ones on the baking show but instead they come out all lumpy and weird. And then you say, 'Nailed it!' even though the cupcakes are bad."

"That's not a real day," said Emma.

"Neither is National Eat an Extra Dessert Day," said Sebastian.

"It is so!" Emma looked at the clock. She

was running out of time. "Hey, everybody!" She jumped on her chair. "It's National Eat an Extra Dessert Day! Who wants a gummy worm?"

"I do!" shouted Mars. Emma tossed him one.

A pack of girls ran over from another table. "Me too!"

"I want one!"

"Meeee!"

Emma threw them all gummy worms before she realized they weren't even in her class. Neither were the twenty other kids crowded around her.

Where was the rest of Mrs. Z's class? Where were all of her maybe-new-friends?

Emma hopped onto the table to see better.

"I'll have one!"

Emma tossed another worm. Shoot! That kid wasn't in her class either. Now everything

was ruined and she wouldn't be able to give Mrs. Z her last worm.

"Emma!"

It was Mrs. Z. Her eyebrows were raised so high they'd practically flown off her face.

"Get down from there! What were you thinking?"

Emma looked down. Her sneaker was in Rohan's mashed potatoes.

"Sorry." Emma got down. She looked up at Mrs. Z. "I brought in gummy worms for National Eat an Extra Dessert Day but then Sebastian said it wasn't a real day but it *is* and then I couldn't find our class to give out the gummy worms so I started throwing them to everybody and now there aren't enough."

She looked down at the bag. It was empty.

"Nailed it," said Sebastian.

Chapter 5
*Tweedle-dee-*WHAT?

Emma thought for sure she'd get sent to the principal's office. They'd call her parents. She'd get a note in her permanent file.

BAD STUDENT. STANDS ON TABLES.

But that didn't happen. Instead, Mrs. Z pulled Emma aside when they got back to class.

"You understand why it's not okay to stand on cafeteria tables, right?"

Emma nodded. She hadn't meant to get up there. It just happened.

"So this won't happen again, will it?"

"Nope. Never."

"Good," said Mrs. Z. "Now tell me more about this special holiday."

"Really?"

Mrs. Z nodded, so Emma told her about the holiday calendar that Aunt Cassie had given her after the twins were born—something to make Emma's days feel special while her parents were busy with the new babies.

"And now that the twins are older, I do special holiday stuff with them. And I thought . . . I thought if I celebrated the holidays at school, it would make me more interesting," Emma said quietly.

"There are many words to describe you, Emma McKenna, but uninteresting is not one of them." Mrs. Z looked over at the classroom calendar. "What if we take a minute each morning to celebrate whatever special day it is? Would you like to be in charge of that?"

Emma nodded.

"Perfect," said Mrs. Z.

Emma nodded again. It really was.

After lunch, it was time for music. Mrs. Berry was waiting at the music room door, bouncing on her toes like Emma did sometimes. Emma wondered if she'd ever accidentally jumped on a table.

"Welcome, musicians!" Mrs. Berry said.

Emma waited for her to pass out instruments. Or maybe she'd have them write down which one they wanted.

Emma found her pencil and got ready to write FLUTE.

But first, Mrs. Berry took attendance.

Then she went over rules.

Then she played them a song on the piano.

It was a long song.

Finally, it ended, and Mrs. Berry said, "I have a special surprise for you."

Emma sat up in her seat.

Mrs. Berry reached into a box on her desk. "I have a recorder for each of you!" She pulled a plastic stick from a tall sock. The stick had holes in it. She put her fingers over some of the holes and blew into the top.

Hooo. Hooo. Hoooooo.

No. No. No.

This had to be a mistake. Emma raised her hand.

"When do we get our real instruments?"

"This is your real instrument!" Mrs. Berry hoo-hooed some more. "At Curiosity Academy, everyone learns recorder in third grade. Then in fourth grade, you can choose another instrument if you'd like to play in the band."

Mrs. Berry gave everyone a recorder.

"Why are they in socks?" asked Wyatt.

"That's the case," said Mrs. Berry.

"Sure looks like a sock to me," said Ayana. Hers was white with blue stripes and had a hole in the toe.

"We're recycling!" Mrs. Berry smiled brightly. "But I promise they're clean."

Emma sniffed her sock. It smelled like laundry soap. But that didn't make her feel any better about playing a stinky hoo-hoo-hooey instrument instead of her flute. All of her tweedle-lee-dreams were doomed.

"Let's play a note together." Mrs. Berry arranged two fingers over the holes and told everyone to copy her. "Now blow gently into the mouthpiece, as if you're blowing on a candle but just to make it flicker."

Emma arranged her fingers. She blew into the recorder.

HOOOOO—SQUEEEEAK!

"Whoops!" said Mrs. Berry. "Let's not blow quite so hard."

Hooo. Hooo.

"Mrs. Berry!" called Synclaire. "Theo is playing his recorder with his nose!"

Everyone stopped playing. Except Theo, who had the top of his recorder stuffed up one nostril. Somehow he'd already figured out how to play "Hot Cross Buns."

"Let's all try that song, but using our mouths." Mrs. Berry moved her fingers over the holes and showed them how to play the notes.

Emma tried it.

Hot cross buns.

Hoooo. Hoooo. Hoooo.

One-a-penny, two-a-penny,

Hoooo. Hoooo. Hoooooo . . . squeeeeak!

"That's all for today," said Mrs. Berry. "Next time we'll learn 'Mary Had a Little Lamb.'"

Emma didn't want to play a song about Mary's lamb. She didn't want to play songs about twinkling little stars or Old MacDonald's farm. She didn't want to play anything on this sad sock-stick excuse for a flute.

Chapter 6

Lizards and Dragons and Sharks, *Oh My*!

On the third day of school, Emma got to tell everyone it was National Be Late for Something Day. Just as she was saying it, Lucy walked in late again. Everyone laughed, and Mrs. Z had to explain that they weren't laughing *at* her. It was just funny timing. Lucy sat down and scowled.

Then it was time for the Daily Scribble.

The Daily Scribble
for Thursday, September 5

What animal should be our Curiosity Academy mascot and why?

I think pigs should be our mascot. Because I can draw them.

Emma tapped her pencil on her desk. The Daily Scribble was supposed to go on for five minutes, but she didn't have anything else to say about pigs.

She looked around for inspiration, but the only animal in the room was Honey the guinea pig, and she was super boring. She did remind Emma of a cooler animal, though.

~~I think pigs should be our mascot. Because I~~
~~can draw them.~~

Capybaras should be our school mascot. I
saw a show about them once. They are
the world's biggest rodents. Capybaras
are curious and friendly. They get along
with all kinds of other animals. They eat
plants and also their own poop.

Mrs. Z's egg timer went off. "Would anyone
like to share?"

Ruthie waved her hand. "Cats!" she said.
"Did you know that cats are super curious?
They're always checking out closets and
boxes. One time my cat Beans got shut up
in the cereal cupboard and we couldn't find
him all day. Then he bit me when I rescued
him."

Rohan flinched at that. Mrs. Z called on him next.

"We should be the Curiosity Academy Foxes," said Rohan, "because foxes are clever and they live around here."

"How about hippos?" said Mars. "Hippos are fierce."

"I am *not* being a hippo," said Synclaire. "What about wolves?"

"Dolphins!" said Poppy.

"Dragons!" shouted Theo. "We should be the dragons!"

"Totally!" Memo high-fived him.

"Actually," said Sebastian, "dragons aren't animals. They're mythical creatures."

"Lizards are sort of like dragons," Wyatt said quietly. "Except real."

"I am *not* being a lizard," said Synclaire.

"Why not?" asked Fia. "Lizards are cool."

Nobody was raising hands anymore, and Mrs. Z's eyebrows were on the move.

"We should be the sharks!" said Lucy.

"No way!" said Ruthie. "Sharks are mean!"

"They are not!" Lucy stood up. "They're misunderstood."

"Maybe we could be the chickens," said Olive. "Chickens are nice."

"Uh-uh," said Synclaire. "Can you imagine going up against some other school in sports? No one is going to be afraid of the chickens."

"I like chickens!" said Thunder. "And I don't want other schools to be afraid of us. Why does everything have to be a competition anyway?"

"We should be sharks!" said Lucy. "Nobody messes with sharks."

"You know what's really smart?" said Carlota. "Crows."

"Yes!" said Ayana. "I read that they can even use tools."

"Does it have to be an animal?" asked Adam. "We could be the fighter jets!"

"Team Cat!" shouted Ruthie.

"Dra-gons! Dra-gons!" chanted Theo and Memo.

"All right!" Mrs. Z clapped her hands three times. "That was a spirited discussion. And now it's time for gym."

But Mrs. Z's class spent the whole gym class arguing about animals.

Later, they bickered through recess.

Memo convinced Wyatt to join Team Dragon. Ruthie and Sebastian chased everyone around with a petition for Team Cat.

Emma didn't sign it. If she didn't make any promises, nobody could be mad at her. She didn't want to be a cat or a wolf or a hippo anyway.

What Emma really wanted to be was a capybara. In that show she watched, one capybara had ducks sleeping on its back. Another had monkeys getting all up in its business. No problem. The capybaras in the video napped with turtles and played with kittens and took baths with puppies. One was even chilling out next to a crocodile. That capybara just went about its life, and everything was fine.

Emma would be the Curiosity Academy Capybara. Friends with everyone.

Well, almost everyone.

Chapter 7

The "Hot Cross Buns" Challenge

On the fourth day of school, Emma got to share that it was Read a Book Day—Mrs. Z loved that one—and also Fight Procrastination Day.

Procrastination was when you had to do something, but you found excuses not to start. Like when you were supposed to practice "Hot Cross Buns," but instead you rearranged your stuffed animals and doodled three-circle pigs and made banana bread with your sisters because they were having friends over and needed more peels to slip on.

Not that Emma did that. It was just an example of how someone *might* procrastinate.

As soon as Mrs. Z's class got to music, Mrs. Berry asked, "How many of you have practiced your recorders?"

Emma didn't raise her hand. She might be a procrastinator, but she wasn't a liar. Most people said they practiced, but when they played "Hot Cross Buns," it seemed like they had fibbed. They all sounded squeaky and wheezy. Like Bongo when he ran around the yard too much.

"That was . . . not bad." Mrs. Berry was obviously a fibber, too. "But I'd like you to practice more. Here's a challenge for the weekend." She handed everyone a paper. "Put your name on the top."

Emma Played a Song for Me Today.

1. _____

2. _____

3. _____

4. _____

"Your homework is to play a 'Hot Cross Buns' solo for as many people as you can. Then have them sign the paper. Whoever gets the most signatures can choose from my Sweet Sweet Music Jar!" Mrs. Berry pulled a big jar of candy from her closet.

"I love those crispy chocolate ones!" said Ayana. "I'm going to play for my mom's book club."

"I can play at the mosque, but do those

have peanuts?" asked Adam. "Because I'm allergic."

"No peanuts," said Mrs. Berry.

Memo raised his hand. "If we're hanging out with a friend this weekend, can we play together?"

"Actually, no," said Sebastian. "She said *solo*. If you play *with* someone, that's a duet."

"Duets are fine," Mrs. Berry said. "Did you have a question, Thunder?"

"It's a suggestion." Thunder stood up. She looked a little nervous. Emma wondered if she knew about the "Ready, Okay" trick.

"I don't think this should be a competition. That stresses some people out," Thunder said. "And we're already arguing about animals."

"Team Cat!" Ruthie gave Sebastian a fist bump.

"Wolves!"

"Dragons!"

Emma couldn't handle another animal battle. "I agree with Thunder. What if we work *together* instead? There are eighteen of us, so if we each play for ten people, that adds up to . . ."

"One hundred eighty," said Adam.

"That could be our class goal," Emma said. "And if we make it, then . . . um . . ."

"Then *everybody* gets candy!" said Thunder.

"Well." Mrs. Berry looked at her jar. "That would be a lot of candy."

"That is a very big jar," said Thunder. "I think you can swing it."

Mrs. Berry smiled. "All right. Consider it a challenge."

"Yay!" Thunder looked around. "If anybody needs help, let me know and I'll get extra names. I have a really big family."

"I'll do that, too!" said Rohan. "I can play for my neighbors."

The challenge seemed fun. Emma would do what Thunder and Rohan were doing. She'd get extra names and then everyone would say, "Wow, that Emma McKenna sure can play 'Hot Cross Buns' a lot."

Maybe they'd forget to argue over the school animal, too. Emma would be the one who smoothed things over with her epic recorder skills and her great capybara attitude.

It was an excellent plan. Emma played a few notes on her recorder to celebrate.

It still hoo-hoo-hooed. But it didn't sound like doom anymore. There might even have been a tiny hint of a tweedle.

Chapter 8
Every Last Squeak

After school, Emma walked to Minnie's. Mom was scooping, so there were no mistakes to eat, but Emma did get to play "Hot Cross Buns" for Mom and three customers. Just like that, she was almost halfway to her goal!

On Saturday morning, Emma played "Hot Cross Buns" for Dad and the twins. Three notes in, Bongo started howling, so it turned into a duet.

Hot cross buns.

ARRROOOOOO!

Hot cross buns.

ARRROOOOOO!

Dad signed his name, and the twins printed theirs in crayon. Emma helped Bongo sign, too.

_____Emma_____ **Played a Song for Me Today.**

1. Lydia McKenna _____

2. Amy Cho _____

3. Rita Sanchez _____

4. Sandy Verity _____

5. Jack McKenna _____

6. MAE _____

7. ABBY _____

8. _____

9. _____

10. _____

"How many times do you have to play that song?" Dad seemed worried he might have to listen again.

"Just two more."

"Why don't you take Bongo for his walk?" Dad said. "Maybe you'll run into a neighbor."

Bongo was up for that. He loved his stroller. He rode along sniffing the air as if he'd never smelled the world before.

Pretty soon Mr. Orlando came out to water his garden.

"Hi!" Emma waved. "Can I play 'Hot Cross Buns' for you?"

"Umm . . . ," Mr. Orlando had already started watering. "Sure."

Emma played.

Bongo howled.

"I bet your plants liked that," Emma said when she was done.

"You think?" Mr. Orlando didn't look convinced, but he signed her paper anyway.

No other neighbors were outside, but Emma spotted someone riding a bike down the street. It was Rohan from her class.

"Hey." He stopped and peeked into her stroller. "Is that . . . a *dog*?"

"His name is Bongo," Emma said. "Want to pet him?"

"That's okay," Rohan said quickly, and backed away.

"Do you live on this street?" Emma had never seen Rohan here before.

"No, I live on Bluebird Lane," he said. "But now that I'm in third grade, I get to cross the street on my bike, so I can ride over here, too."

"Cool," Emma said.

"So." Rohan pulled his recorder from his backpack. "Wanna hear a song?"

"Sure!" said Emma. "And then I'll play for you."

Rohan snapped his fingers. "Let's do a duet! We can play and listen at the same time."

Emma liked the way Rohan thought. She took out her recorder, and they played "Hot Cross Buns" with Bongo howling along. A trio!

"What's that racket?" Mr. Thomas shouted from his yard.

"'Hot Cross Buns!'" Emma called back.

"I could hear it all the way from my porch!" he said.

"Did you hear the whole song?" Emma asked.

"Every last squeak."

Emma looked at Rohan. "That counts, right?"

"Definitely," he said. "Mrs. Berry never said people had to *like* it."

Mr. Thomas was happy to sign his name. They just had to promise not to play recorders outside his house ever again.

That was okay. There were other houses. Emma and Rohan played for Mr. Tanaka and Miss Rose and Mrs. Fox.

They hit the jackpot at Mr. Hassan's house. His whole family was visiting for his birthday. Emma counted sixteen grandchildren!

"That's more than twice what we needed!" Rohan high-fived Emma.

"Wednesday's music class is going to be amazing!" Emma couldn't wait to see how many names they had all together.

"And then we have that cool assembly on Friday," said Rohan.

"Oh. Right." Emma felt a little of her bounce leak out.

"I'm still Team Fox," said Rohan, "but I

also think lizards might be cool. Which animal are you choosing?"

"I'm not choosing anything," Emma said. "I'm a capybara."

"Huh?"

"You know that big guinea-pig animal?" Emma twitched her nose like a capybara and held her arms out to what she hoped was the size of one.

Rohan snapped his fingers. "Oh! I read a book about them. Did you know they even hang out with crocodiles?"

"Exactly." Emma put her recorder back in its sock. "Capybaras are friends with everybody and nobody gets mad at them or calls them names. Not like last year when—" She stopped herself.

"Wait, what happened last year?" Rohan sounded concerned. Like a friend would.

Emma thought about telling him. But the last thing she needed was people at her new school knowing her old nickname.

"I have to go now." Emma turned Bongo's stroller and headed home.

Chapter 9
Team Capybara

On Monday, Emma told the class about National Wiener Schnitzel Day.

"It should be National Crow Day!" Ayana and Carlota waved a crow petition.

"Copycat!" Ruthie rushed over. "We had a cat petition first!"

"You didn't *invent* petitions." Ayana turned to Emma. "Want to join Team Crow?"

"Emma's Team Wolf," said Synclaire.

"I'm not anything," Emma said. "Except Team Capybara."

"Team what now?" said Mars.

"Capybara. They're big friendly guinea pigs who don't argue."

Ruthie put her hands on her hips. "Are you starting a capybara petition?"

"No," said Emma. "But I *do* think they'd be a good mascot."

Too bad for capybaras, though. Emma was *not* getting up on that stage.

On Tuesday, Emma got to tell the class about National Swap Ideas Day. And Wednesday was Hot Cross Buns Day.

Really.

It was *National* Hot Cross Buns Day. Carlota said they should plan a surprise for

Mrs. Berry. "We can march into music class playing the song!"

"Yes!" said Synclaire. "Like the Marching 100!"

"What's that?" asked Adam.

"It's an amazing college marching band." Synclaire pulled her recorder out of its sock and marched around the room.

Fia, Ruthie, and Carlota jumped in line behind her. Emma couldn't resist joining them. Pretty soon the whole class was marching in circles.

Hot. Stomp!

Cross. Stomp!

Buns. Stomp!

"All right, music makers!" said Mrs. Z. Emma thought she was going to quiet them down, but instead, she grabbed a recorder and joined them. "To the music room!"

They all marched down the hall and started playing outside Mrs. Berry's room.

Hooo . . . Hooo . . . Hooo . . .

Hot Cross Buns . . .

Mrs. Berry was so surprised! She collected their papers and announced that Mrs. Z's class had *tripled* their goal.

They all got to pick from her candy jar. Emma chose a purple lollipop.

Rohan chose an orange one. "Great idea making this a team challenge," he said.

"It was Thunder's idea." But then Emma thought back. Thunder had suggested that it not be a competition. Then Emma came up with the team challenge. And Thunder got Mrs. Berry to agree to the candy prize. "I guess it was both of us."

"I'm just saying you have good ideas. You should share them more often." Rohan twitched his nose at her in a capybara sort of way. Like it was an inside joke they had. The way friends do.

"Thanks." Emma twitched hers back.

Thursday was a lot of days. National Video Games Day, Chocolate Milkshake Day, and National Day of Encouragement, when you were supposed to cheer for people around you.

It was also library day, so Mrs. Z gave the class time to research their animals.

Emma didn't need to do research because she didn't want to argue for an animal. She read her graphic novel while Mr. Bloom helped everybody else find books.

She was getting to the good part when he tapped her shoulder. "Which animal do you want to research, Emma?"

"None of them. I don't want to speak at the assembly."

"That's okay," he said. "You can still look up an animal you're curious about."

"Well . . ." It would be fun to know more about capybaras. But Emma was afraid this might be a trick. Teachers and librarians were sneaky like that.

"You don't have to share," Mr. Bloom said. "But check out some of these books, okay? I worked hard to pull them together for your class."

Emma looked up at Mr. Bloom. He was nice, and she didn't want to make him sad. It was National Day of Encouragement, after all.

"Thank you," she said. "I'll read about capybaras."

Before Emma knew it, she was scribbling in her writer's notebook.

Capybaras
  - Biggest rodent on Earth—up to 4 feet long and 150 pounds!
  - Often live in groups
  - Semi-aquatic—spend part of time in water
  - Scientific name: Hydrochoerus hydrochaeris
    ^^ Also called: water hog ^^

That sounded like a nickname Lucy would make up.

Bongo Butt!

Water Hog!

Emma wondered if it ever made the capybaras feel bad. Capybaras were amazing. They deserved better.

The more Emma read, the more she wished she could talk at the assembly. Maybe she should go for it. It was no different than jumping on the lunch table for Eat an Extra Dessert Day, right?

Except it was. Emma hadn't planned to jump on the table and talk to the whole room. She just did it without thinking. It was the planning and thinking that made you scared.

Emma was still taking notes when Mrs. Z came to pick them up for lunch.

"Would you like to sign these books out to take home?" Mr. Bloom asked.

"No thanks," said Emma.

"Are you sure?"

Emma looked at the capybara on the cover. It was very cute. "Maybe just one."

Emma read her capybara book all through lunch.

"Did you know that capybaras live in groups so they can look out for one another?"

"My chickens do that," said Olive. "They squawk when there's a fox around." She looked at Rohan, who was still adding details to his fox drawing. "No offense."

"None taken," said Rohan. "I think chickens are cool!"

"Not as cool as dragons," said Theo, who was walking by with an ice cream sandwich.

"Are you being dragons again today?" Emma asked.

"We are dragons *every* day." He puffed out his chest. "Call me Theofire the Fierce from now on."

Theofire the Fierce licked his ice cream sandwich and went back to his table.

Emma turned a page in her book. "Did you know that capybaras can stay under water for up to five minutes to avoid predators?"

"I bet I could hold my breath that long," said Rohan.

"Doubtful," said Sebastian.

"Time me!" Rohan sucked in a breath and puffed out his cheeks like a chipmunk.

Emma watched the cafeteria clock. After thirty seconds, Rohan's face got red and his eyes got big. Pretty soon he let out a big *PWHOOOOSH!*

"Was that five minutes?" he asked.

Emma shook her head. "Not even one."

"Wow," said Rohan. "Capybaras *are* amazing."

Emma nodded. Capybaras were very cool animals. Totally mascot-worthy. If only somebody would speak up for them.

Chapter 10
The Story of Bongo Butt

After lunch, the class had one more discussion before it was time to vote.

"I hope you'll consider voting for foxes," said Rohan. "Their cleverness makes them great problem solvers, and that's the spirit of our school, too."

"But I also think we should consider teamwork," said Synclaire. "Like the way wolves work in a pack."

"And dolphins swim together in pods!" said Poppy.

Then Lucy jumped into the conversation. She'd changed her mind about sharks and decided to argue for orcas, which were also called *killer* whales. Leave it to Lucy to pick the meanest animal on the planet.

Emma didn't listen to what Lucy said about them. She was too busy pretending to hide underwater like a capybara.

When it was time to vote, Mrs. Z passed out ballots with a list of everyone's research animals—even the ones like chickens and lizards and capybaras that people hadn't brought up in that day's discussion.

"You may vote for *two* animals," Mrs. Z said, "including your own, if you'd like, and one other. The three top vote getters will represent our class at tomorrow's assembly."

Mrs. Z's Class
School Mascot Vote

_____ Foxes   _____ Chickens

_____ Wolves   _____ Lizards

_____ Dolphins   _____ Hippos

_____ Orcas   _____ Crows

_____ Dragons   _____ Cats

_____ Capybaras

Emma hadn't planned to vote. But the capybara on the book cover was looking up at her with big brown eyes that said, "I sure would like to be the school mascot!"

It wouldn't hurt to give the poor guy one little vote. Emma put check marks next to "Capybaras" and "Crows" and dropped her ballot on Mrs. Z's desk.

When everyone had voted, Mrs. Z tallied the results.

"I'm pleased to announce your three class speakers for the schoolwide assembly," she said. "Rohan Murthy will be arguing for the fox to be our mascot."

Everyone clapped. Rohan looked a little scared.

"Lucy Hooper will be representing orcas!"

Everyone clapped for Lucy, too. Including Emma, even though she hadn't heard a word that Lucy said.

"And finally . . ." Mrs. Z paused dramatically. "Emma McKenna, speaking up for capybaras."

Everyone clapped again.

Except Emma. How could this have happened?

She looked down at the book on her desk. Emma never should have signed it out. Then she wouldn't have been talking about how great capybaras were and no one would have voted for them.

Now she had to speak at the assembly.

In front of everyone.

In front of *Lucy*.

And that was the scariest thing of all.

Emma and Lucy *used* to be best friends. They *used* to play together every day. Sometimes they played Ice Cream Factory where they invented new flavors. Sometimes they played Movie Star Makeover and sometimes they played Forgetful Zookeeper Who Let All the Animals Escape. But they always played something.

Then Emma started cheer, and one of her competitions was on Lucy's birthday, so Emma missed the party. That was one reason Emma had an enemy now.

The other reason was coleslaw.

Emma and Lucy also used to play a game

called Coleslaw Chef, where they pretended they were on a fancy cooking show. Dad cut up cabbage for them and then they tossed it all over the place. They even spoke with British accents.

I say, old chap, we need more cabbage for this slaw.

Fancy a cuppa to go along with it?

It was hilarious, and Lucy wanted them to play Coleslaw Chef for the school talent show. But it turned out you could only be in *one* talent show act. Emma had already promised to do a cheer routine with girls from her gym. They couldn't do it without her. They needed her for the stunts. Emma knew Lucy would understand.

Except Lucy didn't. She ended up making coleslaw on stage all by herself. It was very angry coleslaw. Bits of cabbage flew everywhere, and a kindergartener in the front row started crying.

Emma felt so bad that when she went backstage to get dressed for her own act, she forgot to put her shorts on under her cheer skirt.

So when she did her cartwheel, the whole school saw her underpants.

And not just any underpants.

Bright yellow underpants.

And not just any bright yellow underpants.

Bright yellow underpants with her dog Bongo's face printed all over them. Aunt Cassie had them made special for Emma's birthday.

That was how Emma got the nickname. For the whole rest of the year. And she knew exactly who started it. She'd heard Lucy's voice loud and clear.

"Bongo Butt!"

And then the whole school started laughing.

There was no way Emma was getting up on another stage with Lucy in the audience.

At the end of the day, Emma walked up to Mrs. Z's desk. "I'm sorry, but I don't want to speak at the assembly."

"You don't?"

"No thank you. So I don't need this." Emma put the capybara book in the Return-to-Library box and headed for the door.

"Emma?"

Emma turned around. Mrs. Z had taken the book out of the box. "What is it that you like best about capybaras?"

"Well." Emma had lots of things to say about that, as long as there was no stage and no Lucy. "I like that they're so friendly and curious. And I think they're pretty brave, too." She hadn't thought about that until now. But they had to be, to go walking up to a crocodile to make friends.

Mrs. Z smiled. "I think maybe you like them because they're a lot like you." She held the book out to Emma. "Why don't you take this home, just in case you change your mind?"

Chapter 11
Emmador the Bold

Emma put on her tie-dye dress.

Nope.

She put on jeans and her Sloth Racing Team jersey.

Nope.

She put on black leggings, a red T-shirt, and her denim vest.

Nope. Nope. Nope.

She needed an outfit that said, "Leave this

person alone because she doesn't want to talk at the assembly."

But just in case she changed her mind, she also needed an outfit that said, "This person really wants everybody to get along. Also she knows a lot about capybaras, so listen, okay?"

Emma put on her cheer outfit. It was the only thing that made her feel brave.

She double-checked to make sure she hadn't forgotten her shorts.

Then she checked one more time.

Then she looked in the mirror.

Her outfit said, "Here is someone who's pretending she has cheer practice later."

Her face said, "But first, she might throw up her cornflakes."

Emma tried to forget about capybaras for the morning. She tried to forget about assemblies and underwear and doom. But when she got to lunch, *Lucy* was sitting at her table.

Emma stood in the middle of the cafeteria with her hot dog and chocolate milk.

"Are you a dragon today?" asked Theofire the Fierce.

Emma didn't see many other options. "Sure." She sat down.

"What's your dragon name?" asked Memo. "I'm Memodor the Undauntable." He pointed to Wyatt. "And this is Wyvern the Magnificent."

Emma didn't feel very dragony. "Emmador the Anxious?"

Theofire the Fierce shook his head. "Your dragon name should give you *strength*."

"How about Emmador the Bold?" she said.

"I like the sound of that." Theo nodded. "Emmador the Bold."

Emma liked the sound of it, too.

At the end of the day, Mrs. Z's class lined up for the assembly.

Except Lucy. "Can I go to the nurse?"

"Are you sure?" Mrs. Z looked disappointed, but she let Lucy go. Then she turned to Emma. "What did you decide about speaking?"

All day long, Emma had planned to say no. But she felt a sudden surge of dragon and nodded.

Mrs. Z smiled. "I'll let the principal know."

The Curiosity Academy auditorium had three hundred seats, and almost all of them were full.

"Whoa," Emma whispered. Her inner dragon was nowhere to be found.

"That's a *lot* of people." Rohan's voice shook, but when the assembly started, he volunteered to go first.

"Foxes know how to think outside of the box." Rohan said. "Their problem-solving skills help them outwit predators to survive."

Other kids from other grades argued for giraffes, wombats, and dogs. Two fifth-graders gave a presentation on elephants and handed out stickers.

Emma was next.

Her heart was racing and her stomach felt all twisty. But she took a deep breath, pulled out her notes, and stood up.

It's okay, she told herself. *Lucy isn't here.*

"You got this, Emma," said Olive quietly.

Did she? Maybe she did.

Emma squeezed past the other people in her row and walked up the aisle. She climbed onstage and walked to the podium.

Ready?

Okay.

Chapter 12
A Whole Pack of Capybaras

"I think capybaras should be our school mascot." Emma looked down at her notes. "They're the biggest rodents in the world. They eat plants and also their own poop." She was going to leave that part out but changed her mind at the last minute. "I know that sounds gross, but it's super smart of capybaras to know they can get extra nutrients that way. Talk about thinking outside of the box!"

A few people laughed, but not in a mean way. Emma relaxed a little.

"Most importantly," Emma said, "capybaras travel in packs to look out for one another. They get along with everyone. They're —"

Just then the auditorium door opened.

Lucy walked in.

Emma's mouth went dry. "They're . . ."

She took a deep breath.

Ready? Okay.

READY? OKAY.

It didn't work.

"They're . . . they're . . ."

"Really cool!" called someone from the audience. Emma recognized Rohan's voice.

"They *are* cool." Emma took another deep breath.

She could do this. Full out. All the way to the end.

She was Emmador the Bold, after all.

"I also think capybaras would be a great mascot for us because we've been arguing a lot lately. At least in my class." Emma saw kids from other classes nodding. "We could all learn from these curious, friendly animals. That's why capybaras should be our mascot."

"Thank you, Emma," said Mrs. Parker, the principal. "And we have one last speaker."

Lucy climbed onstage and stepped up to the podium. "I'm going to tell you about orcas, which are also called killer whales." She twisted one of her pigtails and took a deep breath. "Orca calves stay with their mothers and grandmothers their whole lives."

This time, Emma listened. And it was weird. Orcas didn't sound mean at all. Except for when they teamed up to hunt seals and made waves that washed the poor seals right off their icebergs. Which was sad for the seals, but also smart. Orcas had to eat, after all.

"Finally, orcas are great communicators," said Lucy. "They make a variety of sounds, including whistles and clicks. You might call a group of these whales an orca-stra!"

Emma couldn't help laughing. It was nice to remember that not all of Lucy's jokes were mean ones.

When the votes were tallied, Emma's capybaras came in second. The fifth graders won. Stickers could be persuasive. So now they were the Curiosity Academy Elephants.

Emma was lining up to go back to class when Mrs. Z held out an envelope. "Emma, could you please drop this off at the nurse for me?"

"Sure." Emma couldn't help bouncing a

little on the way. She'd gotten up on that stage, and people actually liked her idea. They liked *her*.

"Ms. Reyes?" Emma stepped into the nurse's office and almost ran into Lucy. She was watering plants.

"Oh!" Emma stared.

Lucy stared back.

Emma knew she should say something, but she didn't know what. This was harder than giving a speech in front of the whole school. Emma wanted to run. But instead, she summoned Emmador the Bold. If capybaras could walk up to crocodiles, she could talk to Lucy.

"Orcas sound kind of cool."

Emma waited for Lucy to say something back.

She didn't.

She just kept staring.

It was uncomfortable, even for Emmador the Bold. So Emma dropped the envelope on Ms. Reyes's desk and made a beeline for the door.

"Hey, Emma!" Lucy's voice cut through the quiet office.

Emma froze. Here it was. The return of Bongo Butt. Or worse.

She braced herself.

But when Lucy spoke again, her voice was quiet. "Capybaras seem pretty cool, too."

"Thanks."

Emma waited a few seconds to see if Lucy would say anything else. Like maybe that she was sorry. But Lucy just went back to her plants.

And Emma went back to class. Her heart was still racing, but she'd done it. She'd talked to Lucy.

They weren't exactly friends again. They were a long way from that. But they weren't enemies either. And that was something.

Mrs. Z had promised they'd put up artwork to celebrate all the animals. Rohan and Olive and Poppy were already working on posters. They clapped when Emma walked in.

"Second place!" said Olive.

"Great job!" said Rohan.

"Thanks. You too!" Emma sat down. "I was nervous."

"Everybody was," said Rohan. "I mean, school just started. Everybody's scared about everything."

"Yeah," said Olive, who was twisting and untwisting a ribbon tucked inside the cuff of her sweater.

Emma looked around the room. Thunder

was drawing a frog. Steven kept looking over as if it might jump off the poster and bite him. Carlota was sucking on the tips of her hair. Ayana was frowning at her paper and erasing so hard that she ripped it. Fia was fidgeting with the locket around her neck. Wyatt kept peeking inside his backpack, and Sebastian was whispering into his pocket.

Emma had been so worried about her own secret that she hadn't stopped to think about how anyone else might be feeling. But now she saw other people who looked like they might need friends. Like they might need their own dragon names.

Emma couldn't wait to help them brainstorm ideas. Maybe she'd teach them her Ready, Okay trick, too.

"Hey, we missed you at lunch," said Poppy.

"You did?" Emma said.

"Of course." Rohan twitched his nose at her. Emma twitched back.

"You two look like Honey," said Poppy.

"We're capybaras!" Emma said. "Even though we're also elephants now."

"Oh!" Poppy twitched her nose, too. So did Olive. Like they all had an inside joke. The way friends do.

Emma twitched again and laughed. It sure felt good to be part of the pack.

© Tom Messner

About the Author

New York Times bestselling author **KATE MESSNER** is passionately curious and writes books for kids who wonder, too. Her award-winning titles include picture books like *Over and Under the Snow* and *The Scariest Kitten in the World*, novels like *All the Answers* and *Breakout*, the Fergus and Zeke easy readers, the Ranger in Time chapter book adventures, and the History Smashers illustrated nonfiction series. A former middle-school Language Arts teacher, she splits her time between Lake Champlain and Florida's Gulf Coast.

Kate's favorite thing about third grade was the Sentence Box in Mrs. Fox's classroom at Oak Orchard Elementary School in Medina, New York. It was always full of ideas to inspire stories.

katemessner.com

© Kat Fajardo

About the Illustrator

KAT FAJARDO (they/she) received a Pura Belpré Honor for Illustration for their first graphic novel, *Miss Quinces* (published in Spanish as *Srta. Quinces*). Born and raised in New York City, Kat now lives in Austin, Texas, with their pups, Mac and Roni.

katfajardo.com

The Creators of

William Alexander

Tracey Baptiste

Martha Brockenbrough

Lamar Giles

Karina Yan Glaser

Mike Jung

Hena Khan

Rajani LaRocca

Kyle Lukoff

Kekla Magoon

Meg Medina

Kate Messner

Olugbemisola Rhuday-Perkovich

Eliot Schrefer

Laurel Snyder

Linda Urban

Read on for a preview of Book Two in the series!

From
Rohan Murthy Has a Plan
BY **RAJANI LAROCCA**

Mom clasped her hands. "So with that in mind, I want to talk to you about starting your own businesses. First, you need an idea. Who has an idea for a business?"

Lots of kids raised their hands. Mom called on Poppy.

"I'd like to start a baking business," Poppy said. Rohan noticed that her earrings looked like little cupcakes. So cool!

"Great," Mom said. She wrote, "Idea: Baking Business" on the board and drew a little cupcake next to it. "In order to be successful, it's important to make a business plan—a written plan where you think through how your business will work. First, it's helpful to identify a need in the community. Why would people need Poppy's business?" Mom asked. She wrote, "Community Needs" on the board.

"People always need fun treats for celebrations," Emma said.

"And everyone likes cupcakes and cookies," Memo said.

"Excellent," Mom said. "Another thing to think about is how your business will be different from others that do similar things. For example, I draw cartoon images of people in my unique style."

"I like to combine interesting flavors when I bake," Poppy said. "Like blueberry and rose, or green tea and white chocolate."

"And the decorations could be special, depending on what someone is celebrating," Lucy said.

"That would definitely make this business unique," Mom said as she wrote on the board. "Now, third-grade friends, for the next section of our business plan: What kinds of things would Poppy need for her bakery?"

"Flour," said Olive.

"Butter," said Synclaire. "And sugar."

"Decorations," said Fia.

"And special flavorings," Theo said.

"How about boxes and signs?" asked Ayana.

"Great ideas!" Mom wrote their suggestions on the board along with little doodles of each item. "Next, let's think about finding customers. Where do you think Poppy might sell her treats?"

"At a school bake sale," Wyatt suggested.

"Outside, in her neighborhood," Thunder said.

Rohan stuck his hand high in the air. "At the Peppermint Falls Autumn Festival!"

The Autumn Festival was coming up in a couple of weeks on the banks of Lake Bluewater. There would be food—hot dogs and ice cream and cotton candy. There would be music—even a banjo band! And there would be lots of people enjoying themselves outside. It was one of Rohan's favorite things about living in Peppermint Falls.

"We've listed all these things in our business plan—our idea, what makes this idea unique, the community need, what items we would require, and where we might get customers," Mom said. "The last thing to consider is *why* you want to create this business.

Why does it make you happy, Poppy?" she asked.

"I love baking," Poppy said. "It's my favorite thing to do."

Theo raised his hand. "And cookies and cupcakes make other people happy."

"You could use the money to buy toys," said Lucy.

"Or you could use the money to help someone else or a cause you believe in," Carlota said.

That's it! Rohan's mind whirled and swirled. Rohan cared about both the school community and the planet, and the school garden would be good for both. He thought and thought as he doodled on his paper.

By the time Mom was finished and the whole class clapped again, Rohan had decided he wanted to start a business to help raise money for the school garden. He could get lots of customers at the Autumn Festival, and then keep the business going all year long.

Rohan had a plan. Now he just needed an idea.